EGYPTIAN MYTHOLOGY

Osiris and Isis

Tom Daning

PowerKiDS
press

New York

Published in 2007 by The Rosen Publishing Group, Inc.
29 East 21st Street, New York, NY 10010

Copyright © 2007 by The Rosen Publishing Group, Inc.

First Edition

Editors: Julia Wong and Daryl Heller
Book Design: Greg Tucker
Illustrations: Q2A

Library of Congress Cataloging-in-Publication Data

Daning, Tom.
  Egyptian mythology : Osiris and Isis / by Tom Daning.— 1st ed.
      p. cm. — (Jr. graphic mythologies)
  Includes index.
  ISBN (10) 1-4042-3399-7 (13) 978-1-4042-3399-7 (lib. bdg.) —
ISBN (10) 1-4042-2152-2 (13) 978-1-4042-2152-9 (pbk.)
  1. Mythology, Egyptian—Juvenile literature. 2. Osiris (Egyptian deity)—Juvenile literature.
3. Isis (Egyptian deity)—Juvenile literature. I. Title. II. Series.
  BL2441.3.D36 2007
  299'.3113—dc22
                                        2006003373

Manufactured in the United States of America

CONTENTS

Davidson Middle School
280 Woodland Avenue
San Rafael, CA 94901

MAJOR CHARACTERS

Osiris *was the god of the dead. When he was alive, he was the king of Egypt. He was murdered by his brother, Seth. Osiris was brought back to life and became the king of the dead.*

Isis *was the goddess of the dead and the sky. She was married to Osiris and the mother of Horus. Isis kept the pharaohs, or kings, of Egypt safe.*

Seth *was the brother of Osiris and Isis. He killed Osiris so that he could become the king of Egypt. He was the god of chaos, or disorder. Seth caused war and storms.*

Anubis *was the son of Osiris's sister, Nephthys. He helped Osiris rule the dead. He had the head of a jackal, or wild dog. Anubis decided who could enter the world of the dead by weighing each person's heart. He let in only those people whose hearts were as light as a feather.*

OSIRIS AND ISIS

OSIRIS WAS A GREAT AND GENTLE KING OF EGYPT.

OSIRIS TAUGHT HIS PEOPLE MANY THINGS, SUCH AS HOW TO GROW WHEAT.

HE ALSO SHOWED HIS PEOPLE HOW TO MAKE BRICKS FOR HOUSES.

MOST IMPORTANT OF ALL, OSIRIS TAUGHT HIS PEOPLE HOW TO **WORSHIP** THE GODS.

OSIRIS MARRIED HIS SISTER ISIS. THEY HAD A CHILD NAMED HORUS.

OSIRIS WANTED TO SHARE HIS KNOWLEDGE WITH THE PEOPLE OF OTHER LANDS.

WATCH OVER OUR KINGDOM WHILE I AM AWAY.

QUEEN ISIS RULED WISELY WHILE OSIRIS WAS GONE. HOWEVER, THEIR EVIL BROTHER SETH WAS PLANNING A **DEVIOUS** TRICK TO MAKE HIMSELF KING OF EGYPT.

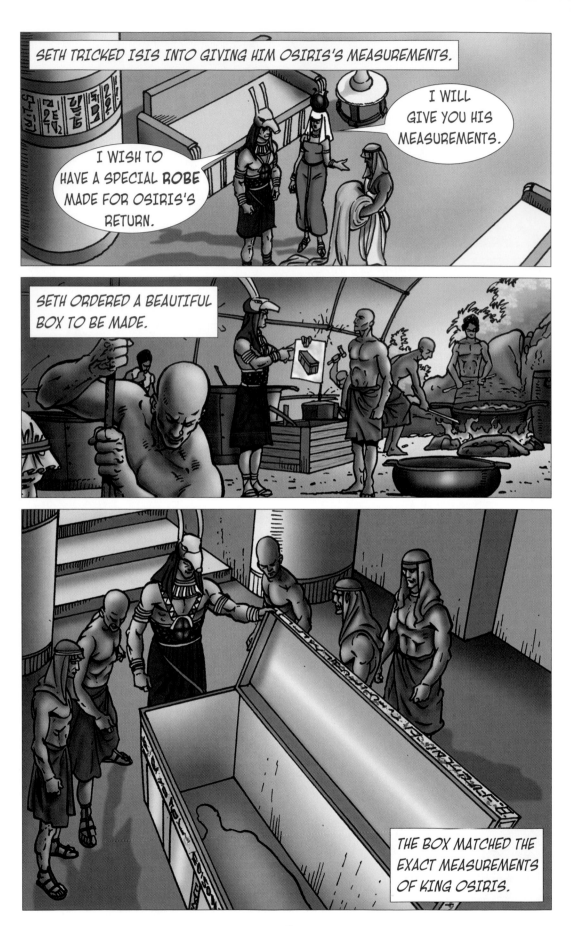

SETH TRICKED ISIS INTO GIVING HIM OSIRIS'S MEASUREMENTS.

I WISH TO HAVE A SPECIAL **ROBE** MADE FOR OSIRIS'S RETURN.

I WILL GIVE YOU HIS MEASUREMENTS.

SETH ORDERED A BEAUTIFUL BOX TO BE MADE.

THE BOX MATCHED THE EXACT MEASUREMENTS OF KING OSIRIS.

ISIS TRAVELED TO BYBLOS.

IN BYBLOS ISIS MET SOME WOMEN WHO LIVED IN THE PALACE. ISIS DID NOT TELL THEM WHO SHE WAS.

THE WOMEN BROUGHT ISIS TO THE QUEEN OF BYBLOS.

MY QUEEN, THIS LADY IS LOOKING FOR WORK.

THE QUEEN MADE ISIS NURSEMAID TO HER SON.

THAT NIGHT THE QUEEN CHECKED ON HER SON IN HIS NURSERY.

WHAT IS THIS?

AWAY FROM MY CHILD, BEAST!

FEAR NOT. YOUR SON REMINDED ME OF MY OWN SON, WHO IS FAR AWAY. MY SADNESS CHANGED ME INTO A BIRD.

ISIS TOLD THE QUEEN HER TRUE **IDENTITY**. SHE ALSO SHARED HER HOPE TO FIND OSIRIS AND BRING HIS BODY HOME.

I WILL BRING YOU TO YOUR HUSBAND.

THE QUEEN OF BYBLOS CALLED FOR THE GREAT TREE TO BE TAKEN DOWN SO THAT THE COFFIN COULD BE REMOVED.

GREAT ISIS, PLEASE TAKE YOUR HUSBAND AND BE AT PEACE.

ISIS RETURNED TO EGYPT WITH OSIRIS.

UPON HER RETURN TO EGYPT, ISIS MET WITH HER SISTER NEPHTHYS.

SISTER, ALL OF YOUR PEOPLE **MOURN** THE LOSS OF OUR GREAT KING.

ISIS AND NEPHTHYS WERE SO SAD THAT THEY BRIEFLY BECAME HAWKS.

ISIS HID OSIRIS'S COFFIN BESIDE THE RIVER.

GOOD-BYE, MY HUSBAND.

SHE THEN LEFT TO RETURN TO HER PEOPLE AND TO HORUS, HER YOUNG SON.

HORUS MET SETH ON THE FIELD OF BATTLE.

FAMILY TREE

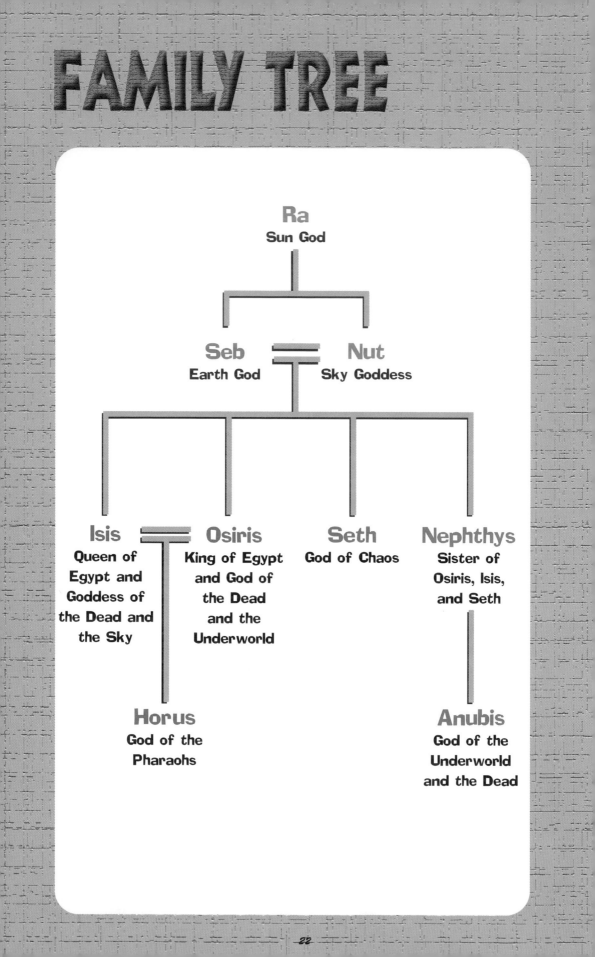

Ra
Sun God

Seb
Earth God

Nut
Sky Goddess

Isis
Queen of
Egypt and
Goddess of
the Dead and
the Sky

Osiris
King of Egypt
and God of
the Dead
and the
Underworld

Seth
God of Chaos

Nephthys
Sister of
Osiris, Isis,
and Seth

Horus
God of the
Pharaohs

Anubis
God of the
Underworld
and the Dead

GLOSSARY

archaeologists (ar-kee-AH-luh-jists) People who study the remains of peoples from the past to understand how they lived.

coffin (KO-fun) A box that holds a dead body.

contest (KAHN-test) A game in which two or more people try to win a prize.

devious (DEE-vee-us) Secretive and not straightforward.

identity (eye-DEN-tuh-tee) Who a person is.

information (in-fer-MAY-shun) Knowledge or facts.

mourn (MORN) To show or feel sadness.

resurrected (reh-zuh-REKT-ed) Raised from the dead and brought back to life.

robe (ROHB) A long, flowing piece of clothing.

scattered (SKA-turd) Threw away in all directions.

shrine (SHRYN) A special place built in honor of an important person.

tomb (TOOM) A grave.

underworld (UN-dur-wurld) The place where the souls of the dead live.

worship (WUR-shup) To pay great honor and respect to something or someone.

INDEX

WEB SITES

Due to the changing nature of Internet links, PowerKids Press has developed an online list of Web sites related to the subject of this book. This site is updated regularly. Please use this link to access the list:
www.powerkidslinks.com/myth/osiris/

Davidson Middle School
280 Woodland Avenue
San Rafael, CA 94901